This book belongs to:

_____

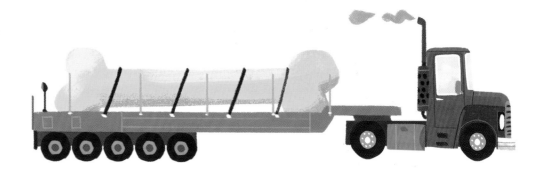

To David, Ellie and Finnemore – M.R.

To Mama and Papa – J.T.

This paperback edition first published in 2022 by Andersen Press Ltd.

First published in Great Britain in 2021 by Andersen Press Ltd.,

20 Vauxhall Bridge Road, London SW1V 2SA · Vijverlaan 48, 3062 HL Rotterdam, Nederland

Text copyright © Michelle Robinson 2021. Illustration copyright © Jez Tuya 2021.

1 2 3 4 5 6 7 8 9 10   British Library Cataloguing in Publication Data available. ISBN 978 1 78344 942 2

RED LORRY, YELLOW LORRY

Michelle Robinson   Jez Tuya

Andersen Press

Red lorry, yellow lorry.

Red lorry, yellow lorry.

Tug lorry. Tow lorry.

Steady as you go, lorry!

Empty lorry,

load lorry.

Straight back on the road, lorry.

Busy lorry, bin lorry. Throw the whole lot in, lorry.

SQUEEZE, lorry! CRUSH, lorry! Never in a rush, lorry.

Lift, lorry. Shift, lorry.

Shove away the drift lorry.

Blare, lorry!

Blink, lorry!

What's in there,
d'you think, lorry?

Sheep lorry?

Cow lorry!

Can you spot the plough, lorry?

Wide lorry... TALL lorry!
Parked behind a wall lorry.

Someone needs a clean lorry.

Just where have you BEEN, lorry?!

Rolling...

dumping, tipping...

lifting!

Ladder raising,

dirt pile shifting.

Climbing, squashing...

spilling, mixing.

Biffing, breaking...

...building, fixing!
Pushing and pulling and
heaving and towing.

The going gets tough and
the trucks keep going.

Red lorry, yellow lorry.
Which one would you drive?
Blue lorry? Green lorry?

FUN BARK
OPEN

JANE'S TOWING

One
two
three
four
five!

On the road all day, lorry.

On the road

all night!

Pick a slower gear,
lorry...

Engines off...

Beep tight!

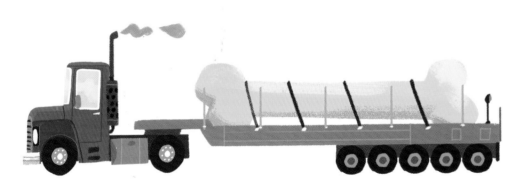

Scan your QR code or
visit www.andersenpress.co.uk/audio/RLYL
for your free sing-along song!